COOKIES AND BURIED SECRETS

A SANDY BAY COZY MYSTERY

AMBER CREWES

PEN-N-A-PAD PUBLISHING

A SANDY BAY COZY MYSTERY

BOOK THREE

I t was a brisk morning, and Meghan Truman pulled the collar of her blue coat to cover her exposed neck as the chilly breeze nipped at her bare skin. She shivered as the salty air flew off of the ocean and ruffled her dark hair, but she did not move from her spot on the beach. Meghan had moved from Los Angeles to Sandy Bay a few months ago, and while she wasn't quite used to the cool weather and dark skies of the Pacific Northwest yet, she was enjoying the change of pace.

"Hey! Meghan!"

Meghan's heart fluttered as she heard the deep, familiar voice of Jack Irvin. She took a long, deep breath, trying to contain her excitement before turning around to greet him.

"Meghan!"

Meghan slowly pivoted to look up into Jack's handsome face. She grinned, her dark eyes dancing as Jack smiled down at her, his blue eyes sparkling.

"It's good running into you. What are you up to? All alone at the beach, huh?" Jack asked.

"I don't mind," she said, tucking a lock of dark hair

behind her ear. "It's so beautiful here. The beaches in LA were always so crowded, and I love having some peace and quiet."

Jack chuckled. "I wouldn't say you've had a lot of peace and quiet since you've been here," he said, and Meghan lowered her eyes, shifting uncomfortably as she stood in the white sand. "You opened your bakery and then Norman Butcher was murdered, and then that couple was murdered, and you just seem to find your way into the middle of it all."

Meghan's jaw dropped. She was shocked by Jack's words, and her dark eyes filled with tears as she recalled the murders that had scandalized Sandy Bay and almost ruined Meghan's bakery, Truly Sweet.

"Hey," Jack said as he saw the look on Meghan's face. "I didn't mean to say it like that. I'm sorry. The murders in town weren't your fault, and it wasn't your fault that your name got tied up in both situations. I shouldn't have said that."

Meghan turned away from Jack to face the sea, struggling to keep the tears from spilling onto her pale cheeks. She and Jack had *finally* started getting along; Meghan had even developed some romantic feelings for him, but his joke was simply uncouth.

"Meghan," he said, reaching out to gently touch her shoulder. "I'm sorry. Let me make it up to you. I'll be at Karen Denton's birthday party tonight. It's going to be a fun time. Let me pick you up for a nice dinner beforehand."

Meghan blushed. She and Jack had been out together a few times, but nothing had ever come out of their few dinner dates. Was this the chance for something to happen between her and Jack?

"Okay," she said, turning back to look at Jack. "Dinner, and then Karen's birthday party."

"Great!" he said, turning to leave the beach. "I'll see you tonight. It'll be something, I promise."

That night, Jack picked Meghan up in his squad car and took her to dinner at *Feast*, a farm-to-table restaurant in Sandy Bay. Meghan had worn her favorite dress, a form-fitting green dress that accentuated her curves and brought out her dark eyes, and she felt confident as she sashayed to Jack's car.

"You look great!" Jack had said as Meghan answered the door. "Let's have a good night."

After dinner, they drove to Winston's Bar, a local watering hole. Jack escorted Meghan inside, and she saw that Karen's birthday party was well underway. Streamers had been hung from the rafters of the bar, and a band was playing in the corner. Jack led Meghan to a stool at the bar and helped Meghan climb onto it.

"Here you go, ma'am," he said, pushing his blond hair back from his face as Meghan settled in. "I'll go get us some snacks."

"Perfect," she cooed. "I made all the food here myself; I hope you like what Karen requested."

Jack returned five minutes later with two cookies in hand. He handed one to Meghan and then took a large bite out of his. Meghan watched as his eyes widened, and he swallowed the cookie as quickly as he could.

"You know I *love* your treats," he whispered to Meghan, their heads huddled close together. "These spinach-almond-quinoa cookies just aren't hitting the spot for me. Did you bring any of your brownies? Your brownies are out of this world."

Meghan's eyes sparkled at the compliment, and she nodded at Jack. "Ssshhh, let's watch Karen blow out her candles, and then I'll go get some of the brownies I brought. I left a whole pan in the back."

Jack grinned, and he gestured at Karen Denton, Meghan's dear friend. "With her insistence on healthy cookies, not to mention the size of her biceps, you would think she's turning twenty-three, not seventy-three."

Meghan laughed. "Hey, if these spinach-almond-quinoa cookies are the secret to having that much vigor and energy in my seventies, I'll take them over my brownies *any* day."

Meghan edged off of the stool and made her way into Winston's kitchen. As she scanned the room for her pan of brownies, she felt a strong tug on her arm.

"Meghan! Sweetie, hello. I saw you walk in with Jack Irvin. How fabulous. I want to hear *all* the details."

Meghan grinned as the birthday girl, Karen Denton, peered up at her, her blue eyes glittering. "We had dinner before your party," she whispered to Karen, pulling her deeper into the kitchen. "It was *his* suggestion."

"Fabulous!" Karen squealed. "I could not ask for a better birthday present. I've always liked that Jack Irvin, and you know I just think the world of you. I'll keep my fingers crossed. Maybe by my next birthday, you two will be a real couple."

Meghan giggled. "We'll see," she said, reaching to hug Karen. "Enough about me. How are you enjoying your party?"

Karen beamed. "It's exactly what I wanted. I don't have a family of my own, but everyone in Sandy Bay came together to celebrate my birthday. It's just *fabulous*. Everyone is here, Winston kindly opened his bar for us, and those healthy cookies you baked for me are a delight. This old lady couldn't ask for *anything* more on her birthday."

After finishing their hug, the two women turned to walk back into the main area of Winston's bar. Meghan had a plate of brownies for Jack, and she could feel her body growing warm as she caught his eye from across the room. Jack looked so handsome in his blue button-down shirt, and Meghan turned to gush to Karen about how happy she was to be at the party with him. Before she could whisper into Karen's ear, however, Karen stopped in the middle of the room.

"Oh my," Karen stammered, her blue eyes large. A stunningly beautiful woman was walking toward them; she had waist-length black hair, enormous brown eyes, and tan skin. A flower tattoo snaked around her right bicep, and Meghan cocked her head to the side as the woman approached.

"Are you alright?" Meghan asked, looking at Karen with concern. "Who is that?"

Karen's mouth opened, and she clasped a hand to her chest.

"It's my… my… my... it's my *daughter*."

2

M eghan gasped as the woman walked right up to Karen. Meghan leaned over, wrapping an arm around Karen, who looked as though she were about to faint. "Your *daughter?*" Meghan whispered, feeling Karen's strong body go limp in her arms. "Karen! You have a *daughter?*"

Karen slowly nodded. "It's a long story," she said, shaking as the dark-haired woman sauntered over. "I don't talk about her often."

"Well, that's a shame," the woman said, catching the end of the conversation. "Why don't you talk about me, Mamá?" The woman stuck out her lips and feigned a pout, but reached forward to embrace Karen. "It's good to see you."

Karen stepped away from Meghan and leaned into her daughter's hug. "It's good to see you too, Sofía," Karen murmured, stroking her daughter's thick, glossy hair.

Meghan crossed her arms in front of her chest, confused at the spectacle in front of her. She had known Karen for several years now; they had been neighbors in Los Angeles, and Meghan thought she knew *everything* about her. Karen had never spoken of a daughter, nor had she ever mentioned having *any* children, and Meghan was puzzled by the scene taking place in the middle of the bar.

"What are you doing here?" Karen asked, pulling away from the woman's hug. "I didn't know you were planning a visit."

The woman sighed. "I wasn't, Mamá," she said, her voice tinged with sorrow as she looked down at Karen. "There were some things I wanted to get away from, and I thought the best place for me was with my Mamá."

Karen nodded. "Well, of course," she drawled. "I can help you with whatever you need, Sofía."

Sofía grinned. "Well, the first thing I need is a *drink*. I've been driving all day, and I need a little something to take the edge off."

Karen frowned. Meghan knew Karen didn't drink, and she decided to introduce herself.

"Hi!" Meghan said, smiling warmly at Sofía, "I'm Meghan Truman. I'm a friend of... your mom."

Sofía looked up and down at Meghan, her dark eyebrows raised. "Aren't you a little young to be hanging out with her?"

Meghan laughed. "I'm twenty-seven, but to be honest, Karen keeps *me* young. She's so fit and in shape, she puts me to shame."

Sofía rolled her eyes. "That's nice. Look, I'm talking with my Mamá right now. Can you leave us alone?"

Meghan was taken aback, but she nodded. "Of course," she said. "I'll give you two some time."

Ten minutes later, Karen wandered over to Meghan and Jack. "Can I talk with you?" she asked. Meghan said nothing, but took Karen's hand and walked with her into an empty back room.

"Meghan," Karen whispered, burying her head in her hands. "I can't believe she is here."

Meghan's eyes widened. "Is she really your daughter, Karen? I didn't even know you *had* a daughter."

Karen moaned. "She's been in a lot of trouble, Meghan. It's not healthy to dwell on trouble, and I try to limit how much I think about her."

Meghan stared at Karen. "Where did she come from, Karen? Who *is* she?"

Karen sighed. "Her name is Sofía," she began. "Her father is a Mexican doctor I met when I worked as a nurse down in Jalisco. I was so young when she was born, Meghan; I was fresh out of nursing school when I took the position as a traveling nurse, and it wasn't even a year after my arrival in Jalisco that Sofía was born."

Meghan placed a hand on her heart. "What happened to her father? Why did you *leave* your daughter, Karen?"

Karen groaned. "Her father is a good man. We were married while Sofía was a little girl. When my visa expired, I had to go back to America, and everything just fell apart. It was a few years before I could get back into Mexico, and by the time I returned home, Sofía was a terror. My husband was resentful that I had been away, and it all went bad. I went home to America for good, and Sofía chose to stay with her father."

Meghan could hardly believe Karen's story, and she took a long breath as Karen choked back tears. "Then what happened?" she asked.

"Sofía was a wild little girl, and then a wild teenager. Her father sent her to live with me in LA for a bit, but that didn't go well, and by the time she was eighteen, she was living on her own. She took off with my money and some of my jewelry, and now, twenty-five years later, she's back on my doorstep."

Meghan's jaw dropped. "You haven't seen her for twenty-five years?"

Karen shook her head. "Not since the day she cursed my name and marched out my door. That was the last I saw and heard of her. Her father's kept me in the loop of her whereabouts; I believe he still pays for her credit cards, and he can see where she's been spending money. I'm honestly surprised I haven't heard from him yet; you'd think that Rafael would have let me know that she's in the Pacific Northwest."

Meghan shrugged. "That's a lot, Karen. Are you alright? Oh my goodness, how hard this must be for you."

Karen looked down at her feet. "I always thought it was my fault," she said, her voice heavy. "If my visa hadn't expired, I wouldn't have had to leave her, and maybe she wouldn't be so wild. Or, if it had gone better when she lived with me, maybe she wouldn't be running away from something now as a grown woman."

Meghan shook her head. "Hey," she said softly. "You are a *fabulous* person, Karen Denton. You treated me like a daughter from the moment we met, and I am so grateful for that big heart of yours. I'm sorry it's been hard with your daughter, but maybe things will be different now. Maybe she's here on your birthday to celebrate you, and to make peace."

Karen's eyes were glued to her purple sneakers, and she sniffled. "I think peace is the last thing she's going to make, Meghan," she whispered. "Sofía doesn't make peace. Sofía makes *trouble.*"

3

"I'm *so* glad we could get together." Meghan gushed as Sofía smiled at her from across the table at Winston's.

It was the day after Karen's birthday party, and Meghan had invited Sofía to Winston's, hoping to forge a connection with the daughter Karen had never told her about. Karen had been upset when Meghan first told her the idea, but after they talked at-length, Karen was optimistic about the notion of her second-daughter and *real* daughter getting together.

"Maybe if she knows you, someone so *fabulous* and a good influence, she will behave." Karen had squealed on the phone as they discussed the meeting. "You are a sweetheart, Meghan, and I'm thankful you are trying to help."

Sofía had agreed to the meeting. She arrived twenty minutes late, wearing a tight-fitting, low-cut red dress; Meghan felt churlish and frumpy in her striped t-shirt and olive pants, but Sofía was nice enough, and Meghan genuinely enjoyed their conversation.

"I know our first meeting was a little awkward, so I'm glad we could have some time to chat one-on-one."

"As am I," Sofía murmured, as she sipped her martini, her long, blood-red fingernails contrasting sharply against the translucent glass. "It was overwhelming to see my mother for the first time in so long, so forgive me if I wasn't quite my best."

Meghan reached her hand across the table, placing her palm over the top of Sofia's caramel-colored hand.

"Sofía," she said, her dark eyes wide as she addressed Karen's daughter. "I hope you know you're welcome in Sandy Bay. I've known Karen, your mother, for several years now, and she is the kindest person I've ever met. I know it was... strange to see her again, but I promise you, she is happy to have you here."

Sofía closed her dark eyes and sighed. "I just don't know," she said, sliding her hand out from beneath Meghan's. "You've been such a doll, Meghan, but I saw my mother's face when I walked in that door. I just wanted to see her on her birthday, and she looked as if she had seen a ghost."

Meghan's heart lurched as she saw the pain invade Sofía's beautiful, angular face.

"Sofía," she said. "Just trust me. I know we hardly know each other, but I know what it's like to be new in town and to feel out of place. Sandy Bay is a nice town, and your mother is a good person. Just give things some time. *I'm* happy to meet you. Any friend... or special person... to Karen is someone special to *me* too."

Sofía tucked a lock of her thick, glossy dark hair behind her ear and leaned back into her chair. Meghan noticed a pair of milky-white pearl studs in Sofia's ears, and she grinned, tucked back her own hair to reveal *her* pearl earrings.

"Look!" she said, fingering her earlobe. "We match!"

The corners of Sofia's lips turned upward into a smile. "Yes, we do," she replied, touching her own earrings with the tips of her long, red fingernails. "Pearls make a woman *fabulosa*."

The two women smiled at each other, and Meghan copied Sofía's relaxed pose, settling into her chair. "So, tell me more about yourself." Meghan chirped. "Karen only told me a bit about you, and I want to hear more."

Sofía raised a dark eyebrow and laughed at Meghan. "You want to hear *more*?"

Meghan nodded, hoping to make a good connection with Karen's daughter. "Of course!"

Sofía took a long breath and swirled her glass, the large ice cubes making little clinking sounds as they crashed into each other. "There really isn't much to know, Meghan," Sofía said. "I'm sure my mother told you that I was a wild one when I was younger. I'm older now, and I want to settle down. I've been a wanderer for years, and I'm getting tired. I want to have a... a quiet life, you know?"

Meghan bobbed her head enthusiastically. "I totally get that." she said, her eyes bright.

"When I lived in LA, everything was just crazy. Sandy Bay is the perfect place to have some peace and quiet."

Sofía looked down into her drink, and Meghan could see her grip tightening on the glass.

"Yes," she whispered. "Life has just been... crazy. I'm ready for a new start here. I just hope Brody stays away..."

Meghan's eyes widened. "Brody?"

Sofía shook her head. "Oh, he's no one."

Meghan leaned in. "Oh, come on!" she coaxed. "I've told you all about my life before Sandy Bay. Was Brody someone special?"

Sofía shrugged. "He was a great love of mine, but he's *crazy*, Meghan. I was in business with him and a friend of his before I got here—they called us the three amigos—but everything just got so... messed up. Brody turned into a terrible man. He was wicked and horrible, Meghan. I was *scared* of him. That's why I left in the first place, to be honest..."

Meghan frowned. "I'm sorry to hear that," she said sympathetically. "Business is a tricky thing. I own my business all by myself, and I've had all sorts of trouble. I can't imagine doing it with two other people."

Sofía closed her eyes and moaned quietly. "It was just so hard," she whispered, still gazing into her now-empty glass. "Everything went all wrong. I just want a fresh start here in Sandy Bay. I want a fresh start with my mother, and a fresh start for *myself*, away from Brody, away from the business, and away from who I used to be."

Meghan reached across the table and lightly touched Sofía's arm. "Sandy Bay is the perfect place to start over. Everyone is so nice, and I *know* things with you and Karen will work out. I'm happy you're here, Sofía. Seriously, I'm so glad we got together, and I hope you know that you can consider me your very first friend in Sandy Bay."

Sofía's dark eyes sparkled, and she released her grip on the empty martini glass. "Gracias, amiga," she said, staring into Meghan's eyes. "I think it's all gonna be good."

After Meghan and Sofía had hugged goodbye, Meghan turned to walk back to her little apartment. She lived in a small unit right above her bakery, and it was only a short walk home. As she walked through the darkened streets of Sandy Bay, her heart soared; she had easily befriended Karen's estranged daughter, and Meghan felt as though she could mend the rift between mother and daughter. As she passed the shops and houses between Winston's and Truly Sweet, Meghan felt as though all was truly well in her life.

"Everything is settling into place." Meghan thought as she turned the corner. Suddenly, just behind her, she heard the thud of footsteps. She quickened her pace, clutching her purse tightly and moving her legs as fast as they would go. Meghan glanced behind her and caught sight of a dark figure only a few steps behind her.

"Oh no," Meghan said under her breath as she moved toward Truly Sweet. "Not again."

Meghan remembered the chaos of her first few days in Sandy Bay. She had been stalked by a dark figure who turned out to be a murderer as she went for a run in the park, and now, she could feel the icy, gripping tug of fear consuming her body as another dark figure walked behind her in the darkness of the evening.

"Keep it together, Truman," she said to herself as she broke into a sprint. She dashed toward the familiar yellow door of her bakery and jammed the key inside the lock. As she stood on the doorstep of her bakery, she looked behind her, but the dark figure had disappeared. When Meghan was safely inside, she peeked out the window. No one was outside.

"Silly me," Meghan muttered as she placed her hand on her thudding heart. "It was probably someone just out for a night-time walk. I am so paranoid. Silly, silly me. I've had too much happen in Sandy Bay already for *anything* else to go wrong."

Meghan sat at one of the little white tables in the dining area of the bakery, hoping to collect herself before venturing upstairs for bed. As she relaxed in her chair, she heard footsteps in the kitchen of the bakery. She gasped as a slim, brown-haired man sauntered out of the kitchen, a cupcake in his hands.

"Hey," he said, taking a bite out of the cupcake and grinning maniacally at Meghan. "I don't think we've met. I'm Brody. I'm Sofía's boyfriend."

4

M eghan's jaw dropped. "How did you get in here?" Meghan asked, rising to her feet and clenching her fists.

"Your assistant let me in," Brody said, wiping a smear of chocolate icing off of his chin. "I stopped in for directions. I've never been here before. I'm trying to find Sofía, and that little short-haired girl who works in here told me that *you* were out with her."

Meghan shook her head. "Lori must have been confused," she said, thinking of her beloved assistant. "I was out at the grocery store. I don't even know a Sofía."

Brody narrowed his eyes and took a step toward Meghan. Her heart lurched. She remembered Sofía's worried face as she had told her about Brody, her dangerous ex-boyfriend, and Meghan's eyes widened as Brody walked closer to her.

"You wouldn't lie to me, would you?" he asked, staring into Meghan's dark eyes. He was right in front of her now; their noses were practically touching, and Meghan could feel the heat of his breath on her face.

"No," she said, plastering a smile on her face. "I don't even know what you are talking about. I'm new in town, you see. Maybe Lori mentioned that?"

Brody took a step back and nodded. "She did say that her boss was new to the area. Okay, fine. I'll see myself out. But if you lied to me… well, let's just say I won't be happy. I *have* to find Sofía."

Brody marched out of the bakery, and Meghan ran for the phone. She dialed Karen's number.

"Karen!" she exclaimed breathlessly. "I need you to get over here. Are you with Sofía by any chance?"

"Sweetie? What's going on? And yes, she just walked in. She said she had a wonderful time getting to know you. You have no idea how much I appreciate you taking time to get to know her."

"Karen, listen to me. I need you to bring Sofía to Truly Sweet immediately. Sofía is in *danger*."

Ten minutes later, Meghan heard as Karen's orange jeep pulled up outside of the bakery. She let Karen and Sofía inside of the bakery and gestured toward the little white tables. "Sit down," she said, her face somber.

"What's going on, Meghan?" Karen asked. "Sofía and I were visiting at home. What did you mean that she is in danger?"

Meghan's eyes widened as she thought about her encounter with Brody. She shuddered as she remembered his sour breath in her face and the evil look in his eyes. "Brody is in town," she whispered.

Sofía buried her head in her hands. "No! This cannot be. I didn't leave a trace when I left him. How did he find me?"

Meghan shook her head. "He was *here*, Sofía. He was randomly in the bakery, and Lori, my assistant, must have mentioned that we were together. He waited here when Lori left and confronted me."

Karen looked confused. "Sofía? Who is Brody? What is going on?"

Sofía's eyes watered. "He was mi amor," she said sadly, her shoulders quivering. "We were in business together with one of his friends. Some things went wrong, and Brody became dangerous, and I left him. I disappeared without a trace and came here to find you."

Karen gasped. "Oh, sweetheart," she said, pulling her daughter close to her. "That is terrible. You should have come here sooner. I know we've had our differences, but I would have *always* helped you."

Sofía sniffled. "I thought I could handle it. It just got too scary; Brody is a *bad* man. I can't believe he found me."

Meghan bit her bottom lip. "I told him that Lori was mistaken, and that I didn't know you, but I think he could tell I was lying. He was terrifying, Sofía. I think you should get out of Sandy Bay. You aren't safe here."

Sofía began to cry. "This is awful," she said, her thick black eyeliner streaming down her golden skin as she wept. "What am I going to do?"

"Here is what you are going to do," Karen said matter-of-factly. "We are going to go home and pack up. We will take a trip together; it's been so long since we've spent time together, and we can go somewhere while Brody is in town. Once he realizes you are not here, he'll leave! End of story."

Sofía nodded her head. "That sounds like a good idea."

Karen grabbed her daughter's hand. "I'll keep you safe," she said gently. "And Meghan… that Jack Irvin is a good kid. He's a police officer, for goodness sake, and I think he has a crush on you. Jack can keep an eye on you until Brody is gone, and sooner than later, things will all be back to normal."

Karen and Sofía left the bakery, planning to leave town

the next day. Meghan slept fitfully, but the next morning, Lori's smiling face cheered her up.

"It's a truly sweet day!" Lori squealed as she walked through the door, her green eyes sparkling.

"Meghan, I hope it's okay that I let that man wait here for you after I closed up last night. He said you had urgent business."

Meghan weighed her words, knowing that her young, sensitive assistant would have a strong reaction to harsh feedback.

"Lori," Meghan said gently. "Next time, let's not have anyone wait for me or tell anyone who I am with. Just give them my cell phone number and let them reach out to me, okay?"

Lori's eyes grew large. "Did I do something wrong? I'm so sorry. Oh, Meghan! I messed up. I'm sorry. I'm the worst."

Meghan laughed and pulled Lori in for a hug. "You're fine, Lori. It's fine. Just give out my number, next time."

Lori and Meghan got to work. They had a hectic week ahead; the Weeks Group corporate order was keeping the bakery busy, and Meghan had even been considering hiring additional help. Business was booming, and Truly Sweet was one of the most popular shops in town.

As Lori tended to customers in the front, Meghan worked on baking pies in the back of the bakery. She bent down to place a pie on the bottom cooling rack in the kitchen, and she heard the tinkling of the little silver bells attached to the front door. Instead of hearing the pleasant chatter of customers, she heard Lori scream. Meghan dropped the pie and ran into the dining area. Brody was standing in front of the counter, his face red and his brow twitching.

"You! I knew you were lying to me." he roared at Meghan as her jaw dropped. "You knew where Sofía was the whole time. I told you it would be trouble for you if you lied, and well, here is trouble."

Lori cowered behind Meghan, and Meghan struggled to maintain her composure as Brody slowly stepped toward her.

"Get away from me," Meghan hissed as he walked closer. "Stay away! I know that you're bad news, Brody, and I will call the police."

Brody laughed. "It will take forever for the cops to get here. Good luck, girlie."

Meghan reached behind her for *anything* to use as a weapon. She felt the sharp edge of a knife, and she grabbed the handle, holding the knife in front of her.

"I said, stay away!" she yelled, pointing the knife at Brody's face. His eyes widened, but he kept moving toward Meghan.

"You're gonna be sorry for lying to me," he said. "And you're gonna be even sorrier for waving that knife in my face. Give it to me."

"No!" she yelled as Brody lunged at her.

"Ohhhhhh!" Brody cried out, flying sideways.

Meghan looked up. Mrs. Sally Sheridan, one of the oldest women in town, stood above Brody, who was now lying on the wooden floor. Her cane was raised above her head, and she brought it down over Brody's head.

"Mrs. Sheridan!" Meghan gasped. "You saved us."

"I came to ask for a refund on these nasty little cookies," Mrs. Sheridan said, setting a bag of cookies on the counter. "I heard this man threatening you." Mrs. Sheridan stepped back to survey her handiwork. Brody was holding his head and groaning.

"That's not how you speak to a lady." Mrs. Sheridan said, glancing from Brody to Meghan. "I'll be expecting a refund next time I come in, Miss Truman. There's too much commotion going on here for me today. I'll be leaving now. You two girls best contact the authorities before he comes to his senses."

Meghan and Lori stared in awe as Mrs. Sheridan hobbled out of the bakery. "I didn't even hear her come in." Lori whispered. "She saved us."

"Yes, she did," Meghan replied. "Come on, Lori. Let's get out of here and call the police. I'm told that this man is dangerous, and he's certainly proved that today."

Later that evening, as Meghan was settling into bed after the hectic day, she received a frantic call from Karen.

"Have you heard what happened?" Karen cried.

"What's going on?"

"The police let Brody go shortly after they collected him from the bakery. They said there wasn't enough evidence. He stormed around town until he found Sofía."

Meghan gasped. "Is she alright? Did he hurt her?"

"She's fine, but she's upset. She had gone to Winston's for a drink before we were to leave on our trip, and Brody found her there."

"What happened?" Meghan asked.

"They had a huge fight. Sofía told me that Brody has a nasty temper, and he proved that tonight. He smashed the windows at Winston's bar, and he broke all the wine glasses in Winston's nice case. He and Sofía were screaming at each other, and Winston himself finally had to get involved."

"That's horrible," Meghan said. "I can't believe he found her."

"That's not all," Karen said, her voice shaking. "Winston told Brody to leave town, or otherwise, he would be sorry. Sofía told me that they started to fight, and she jumped in the middle. I guess it got ugly, and then, Brody finally stomped out. Winston drove Sofía home, and she is so upset."

"Oh Karen," she murmured. "What are you going to do?"

"Meghan, I am a mother," she said firmly. "I have let my daughter down before, but this time, I am going to do right by her. I am a mother, and mothers would do *anything* to protect their daughters. *Anything.*"

Meghan and Karen said their goodbyes, and as Meghan climbed into bed, she felt shaken. Brody's intrusion had been terrifying, and if Mrs. Sheridan hadn't intervened, Meghan could have been hurt. Brody had nearly hurt Winston *and* Sofía, and Meghan felt anxious as she drifted off to sleep.

The next morning, Meghan awoke to her phone ringing. She rolled over in bed, ignoring the noise, but call after call came in. Finally, she answered the phone.

"Meghan!" Sofía cried. "He's dead! He's dead. He was at the bar last night, and now, he's dead."

"Who is dead?" Meghan asked, rubbing her eyes. "Winston?"

"Brody! Brody is *dead*!"

5

"He's *what?*" Meghan asked in disbelief.

"He's dead. Brody is dead!" Sofia screamed. "I wanted him to leave me alone. I didn't want him dead."

"Sofia… what *happened?*" she asked, holding a hand to her heart as Sofia cried.

"I don't know. Mamá isn't home, and I went to grab a coffee in town. I heard screaming and saw police cars as I got closer to town, and then, I saw his body in an alley. The police were covering it with a sheet. He's dead, Meghan."

Meghan was in shock. "Where is your mother?"

"I don't know. Mamá gave me some sleeping pills last night to calm me down, and when I woke up, she was gone. She left a note saying that she was going to the gym, but she still isn't home."

"That's pretty normal," she said slowly, recalling her conversation with Karen the night before. "She works out for hours each day. I'm sure she'll be back soon."

"It's just crazy, Meghan. He's dead, and a police officer called the house, looking for *me*. I have to go down to the station later and talk to them. I can't get ahold of my mom, and I don't know what I'm gonna say. I just *hate* cops, you know?"

Meghan thought of Jack dressed in his police uniform and shook her head. "The police in Sandy Bay are good people. Just be honest and relax. This will all be figured out, I promise. Look, since Karen isn't back yet, I'll come pick you up from the station later, okay?"

Sofia hiccuped. "Okay, Meghan. That would be nice. Gracias, chica."

Meghan arrived at the police station that evening with a concerned look on her face. She had been accused of *three* murders since moving to Sandy Bay, and as she climbed the steps of the Sandy Bay Police Station, she fretted that her name would somehow come up in the investigation of Brody's death. He *had* been at her bakery the day he died, and Meghan's stomach churned as she remembered how it was to have almost everyone in the town turn against her.

"Meghan!" Jack Irvin exclaimed as she walked into the station. "So good to see you. What are you doing here?"

Meghan sighed. "I'm here to pick up Sofia," she explained as Jack's face grew stormy.

"I interviewed her myself," he said, crossing his arms in front of his chest. "Meghan, you've been at the center of two Sandy Bay scandals already. I have some concerns about Sofia and this boyfriend situation. I think you should really let Karen take care of her daughter right now...."

Meghan shook her head. "She can't get ahold of Karen," she said. "She is my friend, Jack. I met her terrible boyfriend. Brody was so scary, Jack. He threatened *me*, and the police just let him go."

Jack's jaw dropped. "What? I didn't know about that. Why didn't you call me? I would have made Chief Nunan lock up that monster forever if I had known he had threatened you."

Meghan lowered her eyes. "I'm sorry, I should have called," she said. "I was shaken up, and Karen was upset too."

Jack raised an eyebrow. "Speaking of Karen, where is she? Sofia said Karen was at the gym, but I can't get ahold of her. I'd really like to speak with her. I'm also trying to get ahold of Winston. Do you know anything about his whereabouts? I know Sofia was at his bar last night, and she seems to open up to you...."

Meghan frowned. "Jack, I don't know anything. Sofia called earlier to tell me Brody is dead. I don't know anything about what happened, but I *heard* how upset she was. I think she is innocent."

Jack sighed. "We'll see," he said. "I'm just glad *you* are safe. That Brody character sounds like a bad dude. Whoever wanted him dead *really* wanted him gone. He had quite a few bullets in his side, Meghan. The murder weapon is missing, and it just all seems a little odd that someone like Sofia shows up, and then, someone dies. That's unlike anything I've ever seen here in sleepy old Sandy Bay, and from what Sofia said, it sounds like she had good reason to say *sayonara* to Brody."

Meghan placed her hands on her hips. "I just *know* that Sofia didn't do it," she said. "Let me help you investigate. Karen *did* say that Brody and Winston fought last night. Brody even vandalized Winston's bar. Let me help you look into that. I want to do everything I can to help Karen and Sofia. Karen has done so much for me, and this is the least I can do for them."

Jack groaned. "Meghan, are you sure you want to get wrapped up in this mess?"

Meghan nodded as Sofia appeared through a door at the end of the hallway. "Sofia!" Meghan waved. "Hey!"

Sofia looked down at the ground. "Meghan. *Officer* Irvin."

Jack frowned and turned to walk away. "Meghan, do what you want. Just know that I have to take this seriously."

As Jack walked away, Sofia stuck her tongue out at his back. "I hate cops," she hissed. "They're the worst. That one was so rude to me. He thinks I did it. I can tell."

Meghan shook her head. "He's a good guy, Sofia. I know him. Just take it easy. Let's get out of here."

The two women walked outside. Karen's orange jeep was parked on the curb.

"Did you find my mother?" Sofia asked. Meghan shook her head.

"No, I just borrowed her car to come get you."

"I can't believe he thinks I did it," Sofia lamented as they drove toward Karen's house. "I mean, we weren't together, and I hated who he became, but I *loved* Brody."

Meghan nodded her head as Sofia began to cry. "I know," she said softly. "It must be so hard."

Meghan deposited Sofia at Karen's house and drove the orange jeep back to the bakery. As she parked, she noticed Sofia had left her red leather purse in the passenger side of the door.

"I'll get that back to her," Meghan thought as she reached for her cell phone. As she walked to her front door, she dialed Jack's number and began to chastise him.

"Jack, she didn't do it. She said that you were rude to her, and you need to chill out. I know she didn't do it. Have you spoken to Winston yet?"

Before Jack could answer, Meghan tripped, dropping her cell phone and Sofia's purse on the ground. "Uh oh." Meghan said to herself as the contents of the purse fell onto the sidewalk. Meghan bent down to collect Sofia's things. She picked up a tube of red lipstick, fifteen pennies, a wallet, and an expired credit card.

"Shoot!" she said, stuffing the items into the purse. As she reached her hand inside of the bag, she touched a cold, hard object.

"What?" Meghan murmured as she pulled the item out of the bag.

Meghan lifted the cold, hard object out of her bag and gasped. In her hands, she held a gold, antique gun.

6

"You told me you had nothing to do with it, Sofia, and then I find *this*?" Meghan yelled as she pounded on the door of Karen's house. Sofia appeared, and when she saw the gun sparkling in the sunshine, her face grew pale.

"Wait. Meghan, it's not what it looks like."

"Not what it looks like? Your ex-boyfriend was murdered, the murder weapon is missing, and you just happen to have a gun in your bag? Where is Karen? I need to talk to her *now*."

"Meghan?" Karen appeared in the doorway beside her daughter. "What's the matter?"

"Karen!" Meghan exclaimed. "Where have you been? Do you know what happened?"

Karen nodded. "I heard," she said quietly, her face grim. "I was out for a long run and didn't see my missed calls until I got home. It's terrible, Meghan."

Meghan glared at Sofia. "I think she knows more than what she told Jack," she said, pointing at Sofia. "Look what I found." Meghan dangled the small, golden gun in front of Karen and Sofia.

"Sofia!" Karen screeched. "You have a *gun?*"

"Not just any gun," Meghan added. "I think it's the murder weapon."

Sofia reached out her perfectly manicured hand and snatched the gun from Meghan's grip.

"Stop it," she said coldly. "That was a gift from Brody. It's worth a lot of money, Meghan, and if you break it, you'll owe me."

Karen spun to face her daughter. "Explain to me why Brody would give you a gun," she said. "Tell us right now, Sofia."

Sofia leaned onto one hip and turned her thick lips into a pout. "He always said that I was his pistol," she explained. "He bought me this from an antique gun shop in Honduras last summer. It's not the murder weapon, Meghan. Just look at it."

Meghan squinted at the gun. It was in perfect condition; there was not a scratch or blemish on it, and Meghan searched for a trace of evidence.

"That's enough," Sofia said, tucking the gun into the back pocket of her tight black leather pants. "I've had enough of this. That cop already interrogated me, and I don't need *you* in my face, Meghan. You're supposed to be my friend. I came to Sandy Bay to get away from Brody, not to kill him. This is all too messed up."

Sofia marched into the house, and Meghan could hear the slam of a door. "This isn't good," she said to Karen. "Jack and I spoke earlier, and he has concerns about Sofia. Now, honestly, so do I…"

"I know," Karen whispered, her eyes red. "I had a bad feeling when she showed up at my birthday party. That girl has always managed to find trouble. I'm so upset, Meghan. First Sofia shows up here, then her ex-boyfriend appears and threatens *you* AND fights at Winston's, and now, he's dead?

It's terrible."

Meghan nodded. "Karen, what happened last night? Was Sofia here?"

Karen shrugged. "I think so? She came home from Winston's and was so upset about Brody showing up and fighting. I gave her some sleeping medication to help calm her down. The last I saw of her was at about nine. I checked on her before my nighttime yoga class. I didn't look in when I got home, so I assumed all was well…."

"I want to believe her," Meghan said. "She's your daughter, Karen. I want to believe her and for her to be innocent. I just don't know."

"Neither do I," Karen admitted. "Neither do I…."

The next day, Meghan's heart fluttered as Jack walked into the bakery. "Jack!" she cried, happy to see him. "I'm so glad to see you. I'm sorry our call dropped yesterday. There were some interesting things going on."

Jack furrowed his brow. "Oh? Anything I should know about?"

Meghan nodded. "Yes, but you look like you have something to talk about. What's up?"

Jack sighed. "I've been interrogating Winston, and I'm concerned that he may have played a part in the murder, Meghan."

Meghan's dark eyes widened. "No! No way, Jack."

Jack nodded. "Brody tore up his bar, and I have several witnesses on record saying that Winston was threatening Brody as he kicked Brody out of the bar."

Meghan rolled her eyes. "Officer Irvin," she said playfully. "Threatening someone doesn't mean that he killed him. Come on!"

Jack stared into Meghan's eyes. "We found some things, Meghan."

"What?" Meghan asked.

"We searched Winston's bar and found some guns. A few of them had recently been used. We can't be too sure, but we think we may have found our murderer."

Meghan's heart pounded. "There's just no way," she said. "Winston isn't a killer."

Jack shrugged. "Our lab isn't sophisticated enough to do accurate testing," he explained. "We're sending the guns off to a bigger lab in Portland. Until we can get more information, we're going to keep Winston in jail."

Meghan crossed her arms in front of her chest. "I'm just not sure you're onto the right gun owner," she said. "I found a gun, Jack. I found a gun in Sofia's purse."

Jack's blue eyes grew large. "You found a gun?" he whispered.

Meghan nodded. "I think Sofia might not be innocent after all," she admitted sheepishly. "I think you should keep an eye on her."

Jack took a long breath and paced around the dining area. As he walked near the window, he cocked his head to the side. "Hey," he said. "Speaking of Sofia, isn't that her out there?" Jack pointed out the window, and Meghan saw Karen's orange jeep. Sofia was behind the wheel, and she was racing through the streets of Sandy Bay.

"Uh oh," Meghan muttered. "She must be going a hundred miles an hour."

"She's about to hit that sign!" Jack exclaimed as Sofia narrowly avoided hitting a stop sign.

"What is she doing?" she asked.

Jack turned to Meghan. "I don't know," he said. "But you and I are going to go find out."

Without giving her a chance to accept or deny his request, Jack grabbed Meghan's hand, and they both dashed out of Truly Sweet.

7

"I lost sight of her!" Meghan cried as she and Jack followed Sofia in Jack's undercover vehicle. "I'm sorry."

Jack gave Meghan a side-eyed smile. "Oh? I thought you were contributing to this investigation, Truman. You let me down."

Meghan blushed. She liked when Jack called her by her last name, but she tried to forget about her crush and focus on the task at hand. They had been following Sofia for nearly fifteen minutes, and her driving was getting worse; Sofia had almost hit several pedestrians, and she was driving well over the speed limit.

"She's up to something," Meghan said as Jack eased the car into the left-hand lane. "I know it. Who drives like that?"

Jack nodded. "It's suspicious," he confirmed. "I want to check out that gun you told me about, too. You said it was clean, but if she's recently wiped it down, we'll be able to detect that."

Meghan sighed. "What if we don't find her? She's driving so quickly."

Jack jerked his chin at the road in front of them. "Look,

Meghan. There she is. I can just make out the back of Karen's jeep. See? There's Karen's **I BRAKE FOR YOGIS** bumper sticker."

Meghan gasped. "She's pulling into that parking garage, Jack! Look! Pull in behind her."

Jack turned the car into the parking garage behind the orange jeep. "We have to lay low, Meghan," he warned. "She's a wild card. We need to make sure we aren't walking into anything dangerous."

Meghan nodded. "Slow down. She's coming to a stop beside that black car. Look. She's getting out."

Jack pulled his car into an empty spot a few hundred feet away from where Sofia was parking the jeep. "We'll watch from here. I have my camera, handcuffs, and gun, if we need it. We'll see what she does. I have a feeling she's up to no good."

Meghan and Jack watched as Sofia emerged from the driver's side of the orange jeep. Her long, dark hair was piled atop her head in an immaculate bun, and she wore a low-cut black dress. A black lace choker wound around her neck, and Sofia sported a matching pair of black high heels.

"She looks fancy," Meghan whispered. "I wonder who she's meeting?"

The driver's door of the black car opened, and a hand-some, silver-haired man stepped out. Meghan could see his biceps bulging out of his tight black shirt, and a gun was strapped to a holster around his waist.

"He has a gun," she whispered to Jack as the man walked toward Sofia. "He has a gun...Look! He's running at her. She must be in trouble."

Before Jack could respond, Meghan tore out of her seat and ran across the parking garage toward the man and Sofia.

"Hey!" Meghan screamed. "Don't hurt her! Don't hurt her!"

Sofia's eyes widened. "Meghan?"

Meghan wrapped her arms around Sofia and yelled at the man. "Leave her alone! I'm here with a police officer, and if you think you're going to hurt her, you are wrong. Stay back!"

Sofia glared down at Meghan and shoved her off. "Get off of me, Meghan."

The man looked amused. "Sofia? Who is this?"

Sofia rolled her eyes. "A friend of my mother's," she replied as the man chuckled.

"Meghan, seriously. He's not going to hurt me. This is Simon. He's my boyfriend."

Meghan gasped. "Your boyfriend? But I thought Brody was your boyfriend?"

Sofia shook her head. "Brody was my *ex*," she said, snapping her gum and shooting a smile to her boyfriend. "Simon was his friend for years, and then we all went into business together. As soon as Brody started getting mean, Simon and I got together."

Meghan raised an eyebrow. "So you broke up with Brody and started dating his friend?"

Sofia nodded. "Simon was nicer," she explained. "Brody could be such a monster, and Simon took care of me. He's still taking care of me. He drove all the way up here to bring me my *babies*." Sofia walked to Simon's car and opened the back door. Two poodle puppies jumped out and started licking Sofia's legs. "I had to leave them behind when I skipped town," she said. "Simon promised to bring the puppies to me, and here they are. He's the best."

Simon beamed at Sofia. "Anything for you, my love," he said, pushing past Meghan to plant a hard, long kiss on Sofia's lips. "I knew that Brody was a threat to her safety, and I encouraged her to come here to hide out. I can't believe he found her already. He was horrible to her, and he nearly sank our business. Now, I'm here to stay. I'm going to keep my woman safe, and nothing bad is ever going to happen to her again."

Meghan heard Jack's footsteps, and she turned to face him. "Jack," she said.

"Everything okay over here?" Jack said in an authoritative voice. "You were driving erratically for several miles, Sofia, and I'm concerned."

Sofia shook her head. "I was just excited to see my puppies and my boyfriend."

Jack frowned as he stared at Simon. "You didn't mention a boyfriend when you were interviewed at the station," he said flatly. "Were you intentionally keeping that from us, or did you just forget?"

Sofia rolled her eyes. "I don't need any more attitude from you. I don't have to answer any of your questions without my lawyer present. Simon, let's get out of here." Sofia and Simon picked up the two puppies and settled into Simon's black car.

"Well then," Jack said as Sofia and Simon sped out of the parking garage. "This certainly makes things interesting."

8

J ack was quiet as he drove back toward town, and Meghan could sense the tension between them.

"Why are you mad?" Meghan asked. "What did I do?"

Jack frowned at Meghan, his blue eyes flashing with anger. "You put us both in jeopardy, Meghan. You ran out of the car before I could assess the situation. You could have been hurt. I could have gotten hurt trying to save you."

Meghan shrugged. "I'm sorry," she mumbled. "I was just excited that we found Sofia, and I thought that man was trying to hurt her. I didn't know Simon was her boyfriend. She's Karen's daughter, Jack."

Jack shook his head. "She's a murder suspect, Meghan," he glowered. "It wasn't your place to run over there before I had given you a directive. And what were you thinking by talking to Simon? He's a suspect now, too. You've sullied the investigation with your meddling. I shouldn't have let you help. This was a mistake."

Meghan burned with shame and anger. She knew that she

had been wrong to jump into the situation before Jack had given her instructions, but she also didn't appreciate Jack's condescending tone. She was an intelligent, competent adult woman, and she didn't like being spoken to as if she were a petulant child.

"Just let me out of here," she said coldly as Jack passed the large, wooden **WELCOME TO SANDY BAY** sign.

"Absolutely not," he replied. "With a murderer on the loose, the last thing I'm going to do is dump you in the middle of the road, Meghan. Give me a little more credit."

Meghan crossed her arms in front of her chest. "I just want to solve this thing and give Karen some peace of mind," she said, fighting the tears threatening to spill from her eyes. "It's been so hard on her to have Sofia here, and she was so upset when Brody made a scene at Winston's."

Jack gritted his teeth. "I know," he said. "Meghan, I know you're worried about Karen, but I have to be honest with you. We're keeping an eye on her."

Meghan's mouth fell open. "What?"

Jack nodded. "She allegedly gave Sofia sleeping pills, and then she couldn't be found for hours on the morning of the murder."

Meghan shook her head. "She was at the gym." she insisted.

Jack shrugged. "I haven't been able to find any witnesses to corroborate her story. According to Karen, she *was* at the gym at a quiet hour, but until I find someone who saw her….And, think about it, Meghan, Karen's life has always been about *Karen*, and now, Sofia and her troubles are here. It just seems like Karen has more of a motive than you'd like to admit…"

"That is enough of this conversation, Jack," she said. "Drop me off *now*."

Jack bit his upper lip. "I can't do that," he said. "I'm scheduled to interview Winston again in ten minutes. You're going to have to come to the station with me and give information about Simon, anyway."

At the station, Jack led Meghan to a small, dimly lit room. There was a large window in the middle of the wall, and Meghan could see Winston sitting alone in the next room.

"He can't see you," Jack said to Meghan. "Just wait here. This shouldn't take long. I need to speak with him, and then you can talk with me, or someone else, about what you saw in the parking garage."

Jack walked out of the room, and Meghan watched as he entered the dimly lit room where Winston sat. Meghan could see Winston was nervous; he was rocking back and forth in his chair, and he couldn't keep his fingers out of his mouth.

"Winston," Jack began. "Are you *sure* there isn't anything else you want to tell me about the night you and Brody fought at your bar?"

Winston shook his head. Meghan saw his body shaking. Winston wasn't making eye contact with Jack.

"Winston?"

Winston looked up at Jack. "I told you, Officer Irvin. When that man left my bar in *ruins*, I was angry, but not angry enough to kill him. I went upstairs and went to bed."

Jack frowned. "Is there *anyone* who can prove that you were in bed, as you said?"

Winston lowered his head. "My wife has been gone for a few years now, Jack," he said. "You know that. I live alone. I don't know who else could prove it."

Jack nodded. "Well, the reports from the lab have come back, and it looks like the guns we confiscated were not the murder weapon. Chief Nunan and I have talked, and you are free to go home."

Winston's face broke into a smile. "Really?"

Jack nodded. "We'll need you to stay in town for the time being, but yes, you can go home."

Winston raised his hands toward the sky. "Thank Heavens! This place has been terrible."

Jack raised a finger. "Just a moment though," he said, reaching into his pocket and retrieving a small, golden gun. Meghan's eyes widened.

"We found this under your bed in our last search," Jack said. "Anything we need to know about this gun before we send it off for testing?"

Winston shook his head. "That's an antique," he said. "It's an expensive one, Officer. I take good care of that gun."

Jack nodded. "Well, I'll hold onto it and send it off. You can get on out of here. Take care, Winston."

Meghan's jaw dropped. Jack walked back into the room where she had had been waiting.

"That was the gun, Jack! That was the same type of gun that Sofia had."

Jack's mouth turned downward into a frown. "That's what I was afraid of," he said. "Those golden guns are a rare collector's item. From what I can tell from the autopsy report, the bullets in Brody's body had to have come from one of those golden guns. There are only a few hundred in the entire *world*, Meghan. They're rare. And between Sofia and Winston, there just happen to be *two* in Sandy Bay right now."

Meghan gasped. "Why did you let Winston go?"

Jack sighed. "Chief Nunan gave me the order. She said that we didn't have enough evidence to hold him. His alibi is shaky; no one can vouch for his whereabouts, and I have a feeling that he is our prime suspect, but I can only do so much, and when my boss says to let him go, it's what I have to do."

Meghan grimaced. "Winston is out, and Sofia is on the loose? This isn't good, Jack. What are we going to do?"

Jack looked down at his shoes and took a long, deep breath. "I think you've done enough today, Meghan," he said flatly. "*We* aren't going to do anything. I think you need to back off, Meghan. I'm worried that if you don't leave this mess alone, you're going to get hurt."

9

The next afternoon, Meghan was surprised to see a missed call from Jack. Things had been so heated between them the day before, and she was not in the mood to be lectured again. Thinking about the murder case, however, Meghan dialed him back. Jack answered on the first ring.

"I need to talk to you," he said. "Can I come over?"

"Sure," Meghan said coldly. "Whatever."

Less than five minutes later, Jack was knocking on the door of Truly Sweet. Meghan let him in, and was happy to see that he had brought Dash with him.

"What do you need?" she asked, seeing Jack's concerned face.

"Meghan," he began. "Sorry if I was a jerk yesterday. I'm under a lot of pressure right now, and it just scared me to think about you getting hurt."

Meghan's heart warmed at his admission; he had been worried about her, and Meghan could hardly keep the smile off of her face. She couldn't help being good-natured, and she shrugged as she gestured Jack into the bakery.

"It's fine," she said. "I understand. I was stupid and shouldn't have put us in danger."

Jack sighed. "I'm going to be honest with you, Meghan," he said. "This case is difficult. I have a prime suspect, Winston, but I have several other suspicious people in the mix. I know I snapped at you yesterday, but I think I need your help. You've been in the middle of so much here, and I think your experiences might come in handy as I sift through this disaster of a situation."

As Meghan opened her mouth to speak, Winston burst into the bakery. "Meghan! Officer Irvin! Good to see you both."

Jack placed a hand firmly on the holster holding his gun, and Meghan stepped behind him.

"What can I do for you, Winston?" Jack asked. Meghan tugged on Dash's leash and pulled him close to her.

"I wanted to bring an invitation to Meghan," Winston exclaimed.

"An invitation?" Jack asked as Winston nodded.

"To the grand opening. I'm opening an antique gun dealership, and the opening is on Friday."

Jack could hardly contain his shock. "Winston," he said. "You were let out of jail, but you do realize that we have not yet caught our murderer? Consider the aesthetics of opening a gun dealership the week you were released from jail after having your own guns tested for a *murder*."

Winston frowned at Jack. "Officer," Winston began. "I'm getting too old for the bar scene and opening the antique gun dealership has always been my dream. My wife and I spent years saving our pennies for this, and I'm not going to let some ruffian who cost me a *fortune* in repairs for the bar, ruin my grand opening."

Jack shook his head. "I think you should reconsider, Winston," he said.

"Officer, I know that you all think that I had something to do with the murder, but I didn't." Winston insisted. "I've always owned guns. Always! I've collected them, bought them, sold them, shown them, and used them to hunt *animals*. That nasty fellow who came into *my* bar and caused a scene? I had nothing to do with that, and proceeding with the grand opening will help show the people of Sandy Bay that I have nothing to hide."

Winston tossed a red and white invitation on the counter and stormed out.

Jack sank down into one of Meghan's little white iron chairs. "This is outrageous," he said. "Now I have a prime murder suspect who is opening a gun dealership on the week he was held for a gunshot murder? I don't have words for this, Meghan. I'm losing it, here."

Meghan softly placed a hand on Jack's muscled shoulder. "Hey," she said, stroking his arm. "I'll help you. I'm on your side, Jack. We'll get to the bottom of this, I'm just sure of it."

Later that afternoon, Meghan was shocked when Sofia sauntered into Truly Sweet.

"Sofia!" Meghan exclaimed. "Hey!"

Sofia sat down and pointed at the chair next to her. "Sit, Meghan. Let's talk, woman to woman."

Meghan obediently sat down.

"We need to talk," she said. "I can tell that you think I had something to do with Brody's death, and I want you to know the truth. There's something I need to say, and I think you're the only one who is going to listen to me."

M eghan leaned closer to sofia and braced herself for what she was about to hear. Ever since she had met Sofia, it had been a rollercoaster of emotions as she discovered more and more about her.

"What is it, Sofia?" she asked, her dark eyes wide.

"I need to tell you about Brody," Sofia said. "Simon is a good man, and he treated me well, but I never stopped loving Brody. Even when I left town, I secretly hoped that Brody would find me and steal me away. I *loved* him, Meghan. He was mi amor."

Meghan clenched her jaw. "But Simon was your boyfriend. You told us that, Sofia."

Sofia shrugged. "The heart wants what it wants, and my heart always wanted Brody. I didn't kill him, Meghan. You have to believe me."

Meghan leaned her head to the side and sighed. "I don't know what to believe anymore, Sofia," she said.

Sofia nodded. "Believe *me*. I loved Brody. That's what I wanted to tell you. I loved him with all of my heart."

Meghan rolled her eyes. "So, what about Simon, huh?"

Sofia bit her lip. "I liked him and his calm and measured approach to life was a welcome relief from what I experienced with Brody. Now, after the last few days together, I feel like I'm really falling for him. He drove my puppies across the country to be with me, and he's so strong and sweet. I think I'm going to stay with him."

"Meghan!"

Meghan turned to see Mrs. Sheridan walking into the bakery. "I came for that refund. Do you have my money?"

Meghan groaned. "This isn't a good time, Mrs. Sheridan," she said, trying to be polite to the elderly woman.

Mrs. Sheridan glared at Meghan. "I don't care what time it is for *you*, but it's time I got my money back."

Meghan reluctantly walked to the cash register and removed a five-dollar bill. She pressed it into Mrs. Sheridan's outstretched hand. "Here," she said. "For you."

Mrs. Sheridan smiled as she tucked the money into the pink fanny pack around her thick waist. "About time. Good. Those cookies were rotten!"

Meghan inhaled. "I hope next time Truly Sweet can provide better service for you," she said through gritted teeth. "So sorry for the inconvenience."

Mrs. Sheridan hobbled to the door. Just before she stepped across the threshold of the bakery, she turned to address Meghan. "Say, you going to Winston's opening tomorrow?"

Meghan shook her head. "No, I don't think so," she said. "There's a lot going on right now, and I think I'm going to sit it out."

Mrs. Sheridan scowled. "There will be freebies there. Door prizes. Your loss, I guess."

Meghan sank back into her seat as Mrs. Sheridan slowly walked out. "Good riddance," she muttered. "Sorry," she said, looking at Sofia. "That was unkind. I'm sorry I said that."

Sofia laughed. "That old bat was nasty," she said. "I hope I don't run into her at the opening."

Meghan raised an eyebrow. "You're going to the opening of Winston's antique gun dealership?"

Sofia nodded. "Of course! I wouldn't think of missing it for the world. Beholding and using a gun is one of the few things that really make me happy. You saw the golden gun Brody bought for me. I love antique guns. The contrast between their beauty and the harm they can bring just does something for me."

Meghan shuddered. "Oh," she said. "I've never thought of anything like that before…"

Sofia smiled. "I feel like I'll be the guest of honor, really," she said excitedly. "Winston asked me all sorts of questions about guns when I was at the bar last week; we talked all about the antiques and the best types to buy, and I think I really helped him make some of his final choices about what to display for the opening."

Meghan felt the color rise to her cheeks. Sofia knew a lot about guns, but Winston was opening a gun dealership on the week Sofia's ex had been killed. "There must be a connection," she muttered under her breath as Sofia stared at her.

"What was that?" Sofia asked.

"Nothing," she answered. "So, what time is the opening at Winston's tomorrow? I think I might just make it after all."

"And I'd like to thank our newest resident of Sandy Bay, Sofia, for her support in the last week in making today happen." Winston said to the crowd. "Karen's daughter is a beautiful, intelligent woman who knows almost a little too much about her guns, and I'm thankful for her expertise."

The crowd clapped unenthusiastically; about twenty-five people had gathered for the opening of Winston's dealership, and the atmosphere was tense. Winston seemed oblivious to the awkwardness, but Meghan could sense trouble brewing.

"This is the tackiest thing I've ever *heard* of." Kirsty Fisher hissed to Meghan as they listened to Winston's speech. "I can't believe he had the nerve to invite us all here to show us his *gun*. He was just in jail. It just isn't done."

Meghan nodded in agreement. Kirsty's former husband, Vince, was serving a life sentence in prison for a murder he had committed several months ago, and Meghan knew Kirsty was sensitive to the current situation.

"It does seem a bit... odd..." Meghan whispered back. "I'm not sure it's something I would do."

Kirsty smoothed her immaculate blonde hair and narrowed her eyes. "Everyone knows he did it. Winston had eyes for that daughter of Karen's since the day she stomped into town on those tacky heels of hers. I can see it in his eyes, can't you? No wonder he wanted her boyfriend dead."

"Ex-boyfriend," Meghan murmured. "Brody was her ex-boyfriend."

Winston waved at the crowd. "I have another special person to thank."

The crowd grew quiet as Simon walked onto the stage. Meghan could see Sofia was confused.

"This is Simon, and I have to thank him for his help over the last six months!" Winston declared as Simon smiled graciously at the people of Sandy Bay. "He is a subject matter expert on guns, and he has supplied me with more incredible pieces than I know what to do with. He knows everything about guns and bullets, and he has been an invaluable resource as I've worked to start this business."

Meghan looked at Sofia, whose mouth was agape. Meghan could see that something was amiss, and she moved through the small crowd. As Simon took the microphone, Sofia exited the stage.

"Hey!" Meghan called out. "Sofia!"

Sofia ran over to Meghan. "Something isn't right," Sofia said worriedly. "I had no idea Simon was working up here in Sandy Bay. I didn't know about this deal. We tell each other *everything*; we're business partners above all else, but I don't know what's going on here."

The color drained from Meghan's face. "He knows all about guns, doesn't he?" Meghan asked as Sofia nodded. "And he hated Brody?"

Sofia's face darkened. "Oh my goodness," she whispered, reaching for Meghan's hands. "Meghan..."

"We have to talk to him right now," Meghan said. "As soon

as he gets off of the stage, we are going to demand some answers."

As Winston resumed his speech, Meghan watched as Simon slipped off of the stage. "Let's get him," she whispered to Sofia as Sofia nodded. "Come on." The two women walked to the stairs, and as Simon made his way down, Sofia reached for his hand.

"Mi amor," Sofia said to Simon. "Come here."

Simon smiled at Sofia and kissed her on the lips. "My beautiful woman." he said, as Sofia led him into a vacant corner, Meghan following closely behind.

"We need to talk," Sofia said, the sweet look disappearing from her face. "I think I know what you did, Simon, and I want answers." Sofia crossed her arms in front of her chest and tapped her toes in front of her. "Talk. Now."

Meghan walked up and stood beside Sofia. "Yeah, Simon. Let's hear it."

Simon scowled. "What is this? Sofia? What are you talking about?"

Sofia glared at Simon. She reached into her purse and pulled out her golden gun, pointing it into Simon's face. "You *know* what I'm talking about," she said venomously. "Talk. *Ahora mismo.*"

Simon held his arms up. "Easy," he said to Sofia. "I had to do what I had to do. This deal came up months ago, beautiful, and I had to take it. I was just about to close it, and Brody threatened to ruin it all. You know how crazy he was, Sofia."

Sofia shook her head. "So he threatened to ruin this deal months ago? So what?"

Simon narrowed his eyes. "I paid him off, Sofia. I paid him off, and he said he would let me do this deal and let us get on with our lives. You two had broken up, and he was *crazy*! He took my money, and then, a few weeks ago, he reached out to me and told me that he had changed his mind.

He told me that he was going to track you down, and that he was coming up to Sandy Bay to ruin this deal."

Sofia started to cry. "So you killed him? You killed him over a business deal?"

Simon waved his hands in front of his face. "No! No! Sofia, please. I wouldn't do that. I was angry that he threatened the business deal, but I was angrier that he still threatened *you*. I *love* you, Sofia, and he was a mad man. He could have hurt you."

Tears streamed from Sofia's dark eyes. "I still loved him, Simon. How could you? How could you kill him?"

Simon rolled his eyes. "*Everyone* knew you still loved him. I could see it in your face every time we talked about him, and getting rid of him not only saved my business deal, but in the end, it saved your life. He was violent, Sofia. You told me that yourself. I saved your life by ending his."

Sofia gasped. "Why? *Why*, Simon? How did this happen?"

Simon shrugged. "You told me you were coming up here to find your mom. It was a total coincidence that my deal was here; Winston reached out to me before I knew this was your mom's hometown, and it all just went downhill from there. I followed you up here from the start, knowing that Brody was going to tail you as well. I wouldn't let you out of my sight, Sofia, and after I heard him screaming at you in that bar—Winston's bar, of all places—I knew I couldn't wait. He had to go."

Sofia spat at Simon's expensive-looking leather shoes. "You murderer!"

Simon narrowed his eyes at Sofia and glared at her. "I've made so many sacrifices for you, and you are just a selfish, impulsive brat. I did what I had to do, Sofia, just as I always do."

Sofia jumped toward Simon, but before she could tackle him, he shoved her against the concrete wall. Meghan gasped. Sofia moaned as her body crumpled to the floor. She clumsily rose to her feet, struggling to maintain her balance in her six-inch stiletto heels.

Simon lunged for Sofia, grabbing her gun and hitting her over the head with it. "I think it's time you and I leave town, my love," he said menacingly as he slung Sofia's limp body over his shoulder.

He turned to glower at Meghan. "From what I've heard about *you*, you've just been nothing but trouble in this town. Now, you've caught me at… a bad time, but we can do this the easy way, or the hard way."

Meghan stared at Simon, watching as his face relaxed into a frantic smile. "The easy way means you'll keep that mouth of yours *shut.* I'll slip out of here with Sofia, and it'll be like none of this ever happened."

Meghan shook her head. "Brody will still be dead," she said. "You killed a man in *my* town. How am I supposed to just pretend like none of this ever happened?"

Simon's smile evaporated, and he bared his long, white teeth as he crept toward Meghan. "So we're doing this the hard way, huh?"

Simon dumped Sofia's unconscious body in the corner and rushed toward Meghan. He grabbed her by the throat, but she jammed her leg into his stomach.

"Oooomph!" Simon cried as Meghan's knee made contact with his belly. "You! That was a mistake."

Meghan turned to run away from Simon, but before she could leave the corner, he caught her by the hair. He tugged tightly, and Meghan shrieked as Simon yanked her long, dark hair. He held her hair in one hand, and used the other hand to turn Meghan around to face him.

"As for you…" Simon raised the golden gun above his head to hit Meghan, but just before the gun struck her, she heard a familiar voice.

"Hey!" Jack yelled as he slammed into Simon. The gold gun went flying across the floor. "That's *enough*!"

Jack wrestled Simon's arms behind his back and looked up at Meghan. "You did it again, Truman," he said, panting as he looked at Meghan with admiration. "You caught our killer. I don't know how you did it, but you did."

"Don't miss me too much," Sofia said, planting kisses on Meghan's cheeks. "I think Sandy Bay is just too quiet for me, but the puppies will keep you company."

Meghan gave a half-hearted smile as Sofia climbed into Karen's jeep. "Adios, amiga!" Sofia called out as Karen drove them off to the airport.

"Sandy Bay is too quiet?" Meghan muttered as she carried the two puppies inside of the bakery. "Please."

It had been a week since the opening of Winston's gun dealership, and despite the murderer being caught, Meghan was exhausted from another Sandy Bay mystery. Jack had arrested Simon on the spot, and Sofia, Winston, and Karen had been fully cleared of Brody's death. Sofia had decided that she couldn't bear to remain in the place where her true love had died, and the morning after Simon's arrest, she booked a one-way ticket to Antigua.

"I hate to say it, but I'm relieved," Karen had whispered on the phone to Meghan. "I told you, Sofia is trouble. She's my daughter, and I will always love her, but she is trouble."

"Hopefully she finds what she's looking for," Meghan had said. "And I hope *you* feel better. Your daughter isn't a killer, and the man responsible for the murder is behind bars. It's all going to be okay again."

Karen laughed. "I was so distraught that I had cut my runs down. I was only running ten miles a day instead of my usual twenty. Can you believe that?"

Meghan giggled. "You are too much, Karen."

"And you are fabulous, sweetie. Thanks for trying to get to know my daughter. Thanks for acting like a *real* daughter to me."

As Meghan stepped back inside the bakery, she felt her stomach drop as she looked at the clock. It was nearly five in the evening, and Jack was supposed to be picking her up in an hour.

"We have to get ready." Meghan cried to the puppies as they wagged their tails at her. "Jack will be here any minute."

Jack and Meghan had made plans to take the dogs to the dog park, followed by dinner at a dog-friendly restaurant downtown. Meghan carefully selected her outfit for the date; she needed to be casual, but she wanted to look nice! Jack had been complimenting her up and down since she had helped him catch Simon, and she was thrilled to be going out with him.

"That's it," she said as she gazed at her reflection in the floor-length mirror that hung in her room. "This is the outfit."

Meghan was dressed in white linen shorts and a black tank that showed off her long, thin arms. She smiled at herself and twirled around, feeling warm as she imagined Jack getting ready for their date.

"It's going to be great, guys." she said to the two puppies as they watched her from their perch atop her bed. "Fiesta,

Siesta, you are going to *love* Jack and his dog, Dash! We'll have a great time."

Meghan took one last look in the mirror. She pulled her long, thick hair into a ponytail, but decided against it. Meghan ran a hand through her dark locks, and she grinned as they settled over her shoulders.

"It's been a *crazy* couple of months," she said to herself, and to her newly acquired puppies. "It's been hard, but at this point, it's all uphill from here. We're off to meet Jack, all is well with Karen, and for once, *my* name wasn't wrapped up in a murder scandal. It feels truly sweet to be Meghan Truman today, my little puppers."

With that, Meghan fetched her purse and placed the little puppies inside. She skipped down the stairs, whistling to herself as she walked out of Truly Sweet, a spring in her step and hope in her heart.

The End

AFTERWORD

Thank you for reading Cookies and Buried Secrets. I really hope you enjoyed reading it as much as I had writing it!

If you have a minute, please consider leaving a review on Amazon, GoodReads and/or Bookbub.

Many thanks in advance for your support!

DONUTS AND DISASTER

CHAPTER 1 SNEEK PEEK

ABOUT DONUTS AND DISASTER

Released: September, 2018
Series: Book 4 – Sandy Bay Cozy Mystery Series
Standalone: Yes
Cliff-hanger: No

Meghan Truman's relationship with her assistant is severely tested when she becomes prideful over a donut recipe she's introduced to *Truly Sweet's* menu. Matters are further worsened when a distant relative of this assistant, with selfish intentions and bad manners, is found dead in the town center.

The local handyman is arrested and put in jail when several witnesses confirm they saw him having an altercation with the murdered victim. Handsome detective Irvin and Meghan believe he's innocent but the evidence against him is too damning to overlook.

Will Meghan's attempt to give her assistant a second chance at restoring their relationship backfire or will a determination not to harbor unforgiveness in her heart lead her to the true murderer?

CHAPTER 1 SNEEK PEEK

"It's a huge promotion!" Jack Irvin exclaimed as Meghan Truman beamed back at him. The pair stood in the dining area of *Truly Sweet*, Meghan's bakery, and Meghan could hardly believe Jack's good news.

"Being moved up from a police officer to a detective is serious business, and I can't believe it just happened to me." Jack explained, his face filled with pride.

Meghan could see the excitement in Jack's blue eyes, and she felt butterflies in her stomach as he grinned at her. She could hardly contain her crush on Jack; they had been on several dates together over the last few weeks, and as she stared up at his enormous smile and deep dimples, Meghan hoped she wasn't blushing *too* hard.

"I'm so excited for you," she said. "This is cause for celebration. How about I bake a nice black forest cake for you? You could take it in to work to celebrate. I'm sure the folks at the station would love some treats."

Jack nodded enthusiastically. "That's *truly sweet* of you to offer," he replied, winking at Meghan as the heat rose to her cheeks. "I love your cakes so much, but you know what would be great, Meghan? Donuts!"

Meghan's dark eyes widened. "Donuts?" she answered weakly. "Are you sure?"

Jack bobbed his head affirmatively. "Yeah! Chief Nunan was just talking about how badly she wanted donuts, and this is the perfect occasion. I know that cakes, pies, and cookies are your specialty here at the bakery, but could you swing some homemade donuts for me? That would be so awesome."

Meghan brushed a stray dark hair from her forehead and wrinkled her nose. "Come on, Jack! Let me make some brownies for you, or even a pie! Isn't it a big cliché for police officers to love donuts?"

"Guilty as charged! I'm just a big cliché, but humor me here, Meghan. Pretty please make some donuts for me? Please? I would be the most popular officer at the station if I walked in with some homemade donuts."

Meghan forced herself to smile. She ran a hand through her long, dark hair, and looked up at Jack. "Of course, *Detective* Irvin" she said, placing a hand on his shoulder. "I would be happy to make homemade donuts for you."

Jack gathered Meghan into a hug. "Thank you," he said. "You are truly the sweetest."

After Jack left, Meghan raced upstairs to retrieve her cell phone from the little apartment just above the bakery. She rifled through her purse, throwing aside gum wrappers, her sunglasses case, and her wallet. "Where is it?" she groaned, tossing the contents of her purse onto the wooden floor.

When she finally found her cell phone, she dialed the number of Karen Denton, one of her best friends. While at twenty-seven, Meghan was several decades younger than Karen, there had always been a strong connection between the two women, and whenever Meghan had any trouble, Karen was her first phone call.

"Come on, Karen, pick up!" Meghan muttered as the phone rang and rang.

Finally, Karen answered. "Meghan! How are you, sweetie?"

"Karen, I have a problem," she whispered, her stomach churning. "I need your help."

"What's that, sweetie? So sorry! I'm on mile fifteen of my twenty-mile run and the reception out here is just awful."

Meghan couldn't help but laugh. At seventy-three years old, Karen Denton was the fittest, healthiest person Meghan had ever known, and Karen was *always* training for something.

"My marathon is coming up next month, you know, and these back roads aren't going to run themselves! Meghan? Meghan? Are you there?" Karen asked, her voice cutting in and out. The call suddenly dropped, and all Meghan heard was the dial tone.

"Shoot," Meghan said. She thought for a moment, and then called Lori, her trusted assistant. Lori had been working as an assistant in the bakery for several months, and Meghan adored her company; Lori was like the little sister Meghan never had, and Meghan knew she could always rely on her.

"Meghan!" Lori squealed as she answered Meghan's call. "How are you?"

Meghan smiled. Lori was unfailingly friendly and energetic, and Meghan loved having her around.

"I have a little problem, Lori," she said, her voice serious. "Jack came over earlier and had something important to ask me…."

"Finally!" Lori exclaimed. "Finally! It's about time."

Meghan cocked her head to the side. "Finally? What are you talking about, Lori?"

"He came over and asked you to be his girlfriend! It's about time! You've been on a handful of dates with him, and even your dogs get along well together! I'm so happy to hear this news, Meghan! Jack is such a cutie. I can't believe he asked you to be his girlfriend at last."

Meghan sighed. She had been thinking a lot about their budding relationship; Meghan had moved to town and met Jack only a few months ago, and while she hadn't been fond of him at first, she had developed strong feelings for him. She *hoped* that perhaps someday, their relationship would turn into something more than just dates at the dog park and the occasional dinner together, but for now, she had bigger donuts to fry.

"That's not what he asked me, Lori," she said. "He asked if I could make donuts for him. *Donuts*, Lori!"

Lori paused. "Wait, what? I don't get it, Meghan."

Meghan took a long breath. "I don't know how to make donuts, Lori," her voice tinged with sadness. "I never trained formally to become a baker! I went to college, and then moved to Los Angeles to become an actress, and when that didn't work out, I ended up here in Sandy Bay."

"But your treats are *so* good, Meghan! Who cares about formal training? Lots of people don't train for things and are successful."

"Lori," Meghan said slowly. "You don't get it. I have *no idea* how to make donuts! I tried once, and it was a total failure! I couldn't get the filling right, I burned them in the fryer, and the sugar melted into a big mess when I tried to sprinkle it on top. I don't know what to do. I told Jack I would make him three dozen homemade donuts to celebrate his promotion at work, and I don't know how to make homemade donuts! What do I *do*?"

Lori giggled, and Meghan felt the sharp tug of rage in her

belly. "Lori!" Meghan exclaimed. "Why are you laughing at me? This is serious."

Lori giggled again. "I have good news for you, boss." Lori said. "When I was a little girl, my father taught me how to make donuts; it was one of our traditions, and each Saturday morning, we would spend time together making donuts for the whole family."

Meghan's spirits immediately lifted. "Lori, are you saying…"

"I'll help you, Meghan. You know I'll help you make the donuts for Jack. It's my pleasure, boss!"

The next two days were a flurry of activity in the bakery. Meghan waited on customers and filled her corporate orders, and Lori worked away on several types of homemade donuts. She and Meghan taste-tested each batch, and after making several hundred different donuts, the pair agreed on the best three flavors.

"My favorite is the toasted coconut mocha dream." Lori sighed as she bit into a warm donut.

Meghan nodded. "Yes," she said. "That's one of the best flavors. My two favorites were the blueberry lemon and the chocolate chai. I think we have some winners here, Lori. You have been such an angel to help me. Thank you so much for your help."

Lori blushed, her small, elfin face aglow with Meghan's compliment. "I was happy to do it, Meghan. Anything for you."

"We'll have to introduce these to our customers at the bakery, Lori. They're wonderful. You've been so helpful, and I want everyone in Sandy Bay to see how wonderful the donuts are."

Two days later, Meghan wanted to eat her words. Jack had been thrilled with the donuts; he raved about them to Meghan, and he even sent a thank-you card and a bouquet of red roses to the bakery. The residents of Sandy Bay had also been thrilled with the newest addition to the bakery, and after several hundred compliments, Lori's ego had exploded in a way Meghan had never experienced.

"They're saying *my* donuts are the *best* thing to happen to this town in years!" Lori bragged to Meghan as they loaded a tray of fresh donuts into one of the display cases. "Mrs. Sheridan told me she wishes that I had started baking them earlier. People are *begging* for my donuts. Begging!"

Meghan nodded politely. Lori's excitement over her success had been endearing at first, but after enduring Lori's endless boasting over the last few hours, Meghan was ready to scream.

"Kirsty Fisher told me that my donuts are so good that I should open my own shop. I knew my donuts were good, but now, I just *know* they're fantastic."

Meghan rolled her eyes. "Lori," she breathed. "I'm thankful you helped with the donuts; you really came through for me, and you know how much I appreciate your help! I just think that we should focus on work right now and maybe chat a bit less about the donuts? They were a great *team* effort, but we have a lot on our plate right now. Let's focus on the task at hand."

Lori narrowed her eyes at Meghan, and she angrily placed the tray of donuts on the counter beside her. "I knew it," Lori whispered. "I knew this would happen."

Meghan raised an eyebrow. "What, Lori?"

Lori frowned. "You're just jealous," she said. "Mrs. Sheridan said you would be jealous, and I can just tell. You're jealous that I made such amazing donuts, and that *everyone* is *obsessed* with them."

Meghan laughed aloud. "Lori, don't be silly," she said. "You helped make the donuts, but I created the flavors and picked the ingredients. This was a team effort, Lori. Let's not lose sight of that..."

Lori crossed her arms across her chest and glared at Meghan, her eyes flashing with anger. "A team effort? Meghan, come on. You may have helped, but I made these donuts with my own two hands. I have *so* much potential. Everyone in Sandy Bay has been telling me that after tasting *my* donuts. Don't kid yourself!"

Meghan stared at her assistant, her lips turning downward. "Lori," Meghan advised. "Please don't speak to me like that. I don't appreciate the attitude."

Lori tore off her yellow apron and threw it on the wooden floor in front of Meghan's feet. "Fine," Lori said. "I'll take my attitude somewhere else!"

Lori turned on her heel and stomped out of the bakery, slamming the door as she left. Meghan sighed. "That wasn't truly sweet of her, was it?" Meghan muttered to herself. She was familiar with the saying that all good things must come to an end, but she never in her wildest dreams foresaw her relationship with Lori ending this way.

* * *

You can order your copy of **Donuts and Disaster** at any good online retailer.

Donuts
and
Disaster!

AMBER CREWES

NEWSLETTER SIGNUP

Want **FREE** COPIES OF FUTURE **AMBER CREWES**
BOOKS, FIRST NOTIFICATION OF NEW RELEASES,
CONTESTS AND GIVEAWAYS?

GO TO THE LINK BELOW TO SIGN UP TO THE
NEWSLETTER!

www.AmberCrewes.com/cozylist

Printed in Great Britain
by Amazon